I SHOULD HAVE STAYED IN BED!

BY Joan M. Lexau

PICTURES BY
SYD HOFF

HARPER & ROW, PUBLISHERS

For Danny

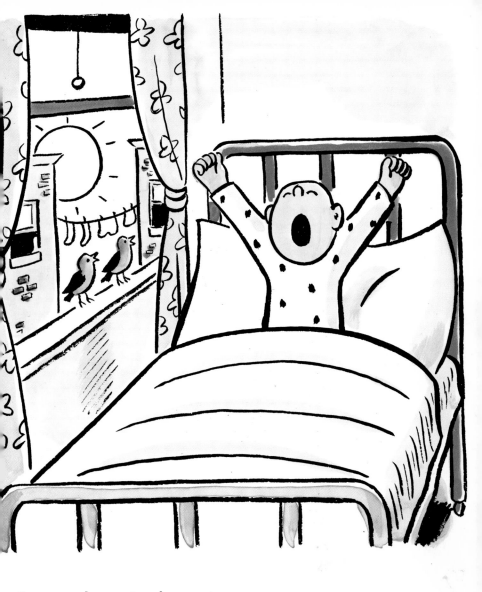

Some days it doesn't pay to get up.
Some days you can't do anything right.
One day I woke up.
The sun was shining.
Birds were singing.

I got dressed. I put on my shoes.
I tied the shoelaces.
The shoes were on the wrong feet.
When I untied the shoelaces, I made two knots.

So I left the shoes on the wrong feet.
I went down to breakfast.

"Good morning, dear," said my mother.
"Why are you wearing your Cub Scout suit?
Tomorrow is Cub Scout day."

"Good morning, Sam," said my father.
"Your shoes are on the wrong feet.
What's the matter with you today?
This isn't like you."

9

I got dressed all over again.
When I tried to untie the shoelaces,
they broke.
I put the shoes on the right feet.
I went down again to breakfast.

"Not so much sugar on your cereal, dear,"
my mother said.
"I like it this way," I said.
I put some more sugar on my cereal.

At the bottom it was all soggy sugar.
I ate it all up. It was terrible.

I went to call for Albert.
Good old Albert. My best friend.
"Albert, hey, Albert,"
I yelled at his window.

"Albert left. It's late,"
his mother said.
That Albert. Some friend!

I took off for school.
I saw a nickel in the street.
"Good," I said.
"Something good at last."

I went over to pick it up.
My foot kicked it into a sewer.
"Boy, I should have stayed in bed," I said.

I got to school when the first bell rang.
"Here comes Sam the snail," Albert said.
"What took you so long?"

I threw a notebook at him.
He ducked.
The notebook hit Amy Lou.

"You could have killed me,"
Amy Lou said. "I'm going to tell."
She ran into the school.

I ran after her.

"Amy Lou," I said.

"Amy Lou, Amy Lou, Amy Lou."

Amy Lou went into our room.
"Sam tried to kill me!" she yelled.

The teacher wasn't there.
So everybody ran around the room.
"Watch me," I said.
"Watch how fast I can go."

I turned around and around and around,
faster and faster.

The second bell rang.
Everybody sat down.

Everybody but me.
I fell down.
The teacher came in.

"Well, Sam?" said the teacher.
"I got dizzy," I said.

"Oh. Go see the nurse," said the teacher.
So I did.

Boy, was the nurse mad
when she found out why I got dizzy.
She told me off.
She gave me a note for my teacher.

The teacher told me off too.
She told me to open my reader
and read.

I read, "Bob walked down the dark street.
He was getting colder and colder.
By and by he was a snowman."

Everybody laughed.

"He **saw** a snowman," said the teacher.

"Maybe you are still dizzy, Sam.

Amy Lou, it is your turn."

Amy Lou read it right.
She always does.
Albert gave me a note.

I opened it up.

The teacher saw it.

"Read the note out loud," she said.

What could I do? I read it out loud.
It said: "Can you read this fast?
Eye yam. Eye yam.
Eye ree lee yam.
Eye man ut."

Everybody laughed.
I didn't look at Albert.
"You read that very well," said the teacher.
"But after this when you and Albert
have something to say, say it to all of us.
No more notes."

I thought lunchtime would never come.
But at last it did.
I didn't wait for Albert.
"Sam, Albert is calling you," Amy Lou said.
"Albert?" I said. "Who is Albert?
I don't know any Albert."

36

I ran all the way home.
I said over and over,
"I should have stayed in bed.
I should have stayed in bed."

When I got home I said,
"Why not? It can only help.
Things can't get any worse."
So I went to my room.
I put on my pajamas.

38

I went to bed and counted
to one hundred.
"I'll call the doctor," my mother said.
"Now I know something is the matter."

"I'm all right," I said.

"I'm starting the day over."

"Oh," said my mother.

She looked at me as if I were crazy.

But she didn't call the doctor.

I got up and put on my robe and slippers.
I asked for some cereal.
I put just a little sugar on it.

Then I got dressed and ran to school.
I didn't see Albert.
I heard the first bell ring.
I heard the second bell ring.
Everybody was in school.

No, not everybody.

There was Albert by the door.

"You're late," he said.

"Well, so are you," I said.

"I know," Albert said. "I saw you coming,
so I waited for you.
We can both stay after school."
Good old Albert.
Good old best friend Albert.

We went into our room.

"Sam and Albert are late," Amy Lou said.

"So I see," said the teacher.

"They'll have to stay after school,
won't they?" said Amy Lou.

"Yes, they will," said the teacher.

"You know what?" said Amy Lou.
"You know what?
Sam has his slippers on!"
Everybody laughed.
What a crazy day.

"Amy Lou," said the teacher,
"you will have to stay after school.
You talk too much."

I looked at Albert.
Albert looked at me.
It didn't look like such
a bad day after all.